FRESH GIRLS

Evelyn Lau was born in Vancouver in 1971. At the age of seventeen, after living on the streets of Vancouver for two years, she wrote the bestselling *Runaway: Diary of a Street Kid*. In 1992 she became the youngest poet ever to be nominated for Canada's Governor General's Award for her second poetry collection, *Oedipal Dreams*. She lives in Vancouver.

Evelyn Lau

FRESH
GIRLS

Minerva

A Minerva Paperback
FRESH GIRLS

First published in Great Britain 1994
in this Minerva edition
by Mandarin Paperbacks
an imprint of Reed Consumer Books Ltd
Michelin House, 81 Fulham Road, London SW3 6RB
and Auckland, Melbourne, Singapore and Toronto

Copyright © 1993 by Evelyn Lau
The author has asserted her moral rights

A CIP catalogue record for this title
is available from the British Library
ISBN 0 7493 9620 2

Printed and bound in Great Britain
by Cox & Wyman Ltd, Reading, Berkshire

Acknowledgements

Some of these stories first appeared in a slightly different form in the following publications: 'Fresh Girls' (under the title 'Twenty') in *Books in Canada*; 'Marriage' in *NeWest Review*; 'Mercy' in *Left Bank*; 'The Apartments' in *Descant*; 'Glass' in *Vancouver Magazine* and *Many Mouthed-Birds: Contemporary Writing by Chinese Canadians*.

'The One Day: A Poem in Three Parts' by Donald Hall, copyright © 1988 by Donald Hall. Reprinted by permission of Ticknor & Fields / Houghton Mifflin Co.

'Do not go gentle into that good night' from *The Poems* by Dylan Thomas. Reprinted by permission of J. M. Dent & Sons Ltd.

Special thanks to Crawford Kilian for reading these stories first, Chris Napolitano at *Playboy* for his encouragement and advice, Maya Mavjee and Iris Skeoch at HarperCollins for their sensitivity and direction, and Doug Coupland for finding the right title.

The world is a bed.

—Donald Hall
from "The One Day: A Poem in Three Parts"

FRESH GIRLS

Carol in the bathroom, holding her hair with one hand and a mascara wand with the other, her face lopsided in the mirror on the medicine cabinet. Her face floating alongside cherry-red mouthwash, dental floss, old razors. Carol fixing her honey hair and saying, "You don't think I'm neurotic, do you? Do you?" . . . coming out into the living room with the zipper teeth of the makeup bag between her fingers, smiling a girl's smile. She's twenty-four — same age as Jane at the massage parlor, bowing her head in the hallway when she thought no one was looking, after that old guy left. Looks like he took more than he paid for. Jane ran an escort agency at twenty, now she's washed up, sits in the back room all day waiting for a faithful regular while the other girls come and go. More blondes these days, making

up their pale eyes at the table, smoking the other girls' cigarettes, reading trash. Jane watches. She's starting to get a
curl to her lip, like she knows too much, but she's not bad-
looking in regular clothes, when she changes into a sweater
and jeans to buy soup or cigarettes or condoms down the
street. She's got freckles on her shoulders, sort of cute.
Looks better when she washes her makeup off, but in work
gear — the blue eyeliner, the tight white dress with the
chiffon thing along the neck that she ribbons into her hair
— Jane looks worn out. Yeah, even though her room is the
one with the little pink rosebuds on the shade over the
lamp by the bed.

Carol's not like that, she hasn't done it long enough. Sitting on the floor, poking at herself with the needle, smear-
ing a trickle of blood with the back of her hand onto her
thigh, onto that dress she's borrowed from somewhere, a
purple mini with flowers. Pretty legs, hair falling into her
eyes; she's not even sweating, though she's been poking for
the last twenty minutes. She's even made one up for me, it's
sitting on the overturned cardboard box Mark calls a coffee
table. Pale gold liquid and then the squirt of her blood in
the syringe, like a curly hair. I look at it, look back at her,
wait to get desperate enough.

"Mark, I need five bucks for pantyhose," Carol says.

She looks up and the lamplight hits her face and her
hair and the hardwood floor. They're all the same color,
honey, and her eyes blink and her teeth show and Mark

goes scrambling. She's one of those you can't turn down, you can smell the freshness on her, like she just took a shower and dusted off with baby powder. Like she just took a walk through a forest. Monica will hate her; chain-smoking and bitching in the back room, one leg up on the arm of that ancient couch, magazines and science-fiction books and romance novels with torn-off covers stacked behind her. Eating chicken soup out of a cup and pulling at her styled bangs in the mirror on the table; tinted so blonde she's gone gray in parts, the parts that aren't shimmering with Grease in the light.

"New girls, they come; new girls all the time," Monica mutters, exhaling angrily. "How am I supposed to make a living? Tell me. First you, then the redhead, then that skinny blonde, she's got an accent too, my God! How am I going to get business? Not so many men, I have to sit here all afternoon, waiting and waiting . . ."

Monica's red lips pucker with hatred, and then the doorbell rings and she puts her feet in high heels, pulls at a curve of hair in the hall mirror, grabs up condoms. She knows he'll want a new girl, whoever he is. The men can tell the ones who've been here long, they smell like the back room, five ashtrays operating at once and the taste of packaged soup on their tongues.

Monica, too, looks not bad when the day's over and she's changed into a man's shirt and little pink shorts, examining her face in the mirror in front of me, carefully wiping off the last of the foundation and brushing out her hair before leaving to pick up her kid. She makes it my turn to clean the bathroom, though, and for a moment I hate her. It's easy to turn to hate behind the boarded-up windows of this place, each room with its lamp dusty with red light so everyone looks good, even sometimes a man, so pale and smooth on the bed it's like being with a baby, its face not yet formed.

"Thanks, Mark," says Carol.

She's rounding the hallway, a package of pantyhose from the grocery store down the street in her hands, her face a bright dazzle. She turns to me and grins for a minute.

"Hey, isn't it weird walking down the street when you're stoned? Like, it's like everyone knows, and they can all tell, and you're scared you're showing it somehow, like they can tell just by looking at you. They all look at you funny, except for the guy who whistled at me. He was standing on his balcony. He was real cute, I wonder why girls can't whistle at guys too? And there was this cop car down the street, the cop inside looked at me real funny . . ."

She's tearing open the package and chattering, but I hardly notice, my arm is turned up on the couch, Mark is telling me to pump my hand and saying "Good, good girl, that's it, there it is," and I'm leaning back against the back of the sofa real fast, tasting the taste of it come up in my throat, like silver or copper or one of those metals, and that slivered feeling all along the back of my neck and shoulders, where it'll hurt the next morning.

♦   ♦   ♦

At the massage parlor I spend a lot of time in the back room too, but that doesn't matter, I have other people. There's a doctor, for example, who calls me every few weeks from Medicine Hat, Alberta. "I want to fuck your pussy all night," he says, and then he flies down for some physicians' conference and I find him on his hotel bed, waiting. He looks at me after I come back from the bathroom with half my makeup gone and smiles and says, "You're still pretty," as if he expected somebody else to be behind the face I put on for him.

To him, and others, I'm still in my Lolita years, but I have a birthday coming up soon. I'll be twenty, and what then? The back room is getting too small, and even the owner's tiring of the pretty girls with their daddy complexes curled up next to the desk where he balances the books and takes half their money; the girls who pull up their skirts and tuck their naked legs beneath them on the chair and fiddle with their long curly hair, pouting — "So, Daddy, should I get it cut? I was thinking maybe I'd get it cut next time, all these split ends, look . . ." while they dangle a waterfall of gorgeous hair in front of him. Everyone wants to be pretty for Mario, he takes their money and lets them sit in the back room when they get old, twenty-four, twenty-five. Lets them eat chicken soup and buy condoms for the other girls and take in a few hairy, smelly regulars wearing checked pants and bad ties. Mario's wife comes in then with her freckled legs, wearing a red dress, tilting her head to one side and saying "No, don't cut it, that'll be bad for business," and the girls lid their eyes and put on older mouths, the kind of mouths that say contempt and knowing, but they say, "Well, okay," and Mario continues to work hard over the ledgers.

But to some men I'm still a baby girl. That's what he calls me, the rich old man in his apartment with the blackened windows, "Baby Girl," he says, "You're still a Baby Girl," and I think I've never heard words so sweet. He calls me nights when he's drunk. He never touches me, that one, only wants me to sit on his silk-covered couch in that incredible room with one wall nothing but a mirror, like a pond of ice, and the grand piano with red roses in a crystal vase on top. The old man in his blankets smokes Silk Cuts and asks me to light the oil lamp on the table. I turn it up too high, so the flame swirls a black mark onto the ceiling. He's getting worse. One night when I go to pee I see he's vomited up his dinner in the toilet, cut green beans floating in the bowl with rice or some gelatinous white substance; he hasn't bothered to flush the toilet. But he likes his Rusty Nails the way I make them — clumsily, "Like a woman," he says, "women never know how to make drinks." I bring them in to him sloshing over the side of the glass, half a cup of Drambuie, half a cup of scotch, no ice, spilling over. He smiles weakly and looks at me in the mirror and says I look good or bad, pick a week, I turn around and smooth some swatch of material over my belly and say, "I'm getting fat," and he says "Yes," and then "No, no, you're perfect, you're just a Baby Girl." And I swell inside, a golden feeling.

"I like you," he says, "that's a real compliment, I don't usually like anyone."

But the cab drivers chuckle when I leave, clanging the iron gate behind me: "That old guy's quite a character, you know, he's got working girls coming out of his apartment most every night."

I know. I know about the girl who comes over from the top massage parlor in town, how she lies in the chaise longue and what he does to her. But he never does anything to me and that's good enough. Nights I sit by the phone waiting for him to get drunk so he'll call me, and I can go down to the secret address via certain cab drivers, tripping through the maze of gates and gardens and the exclusive apartments he lives in. He'll be drunk and fiddling with the grandfather clock in the hallway, offering me a drink and telling me to make it myself. As long as I listen 'til three, four in the morning and give him a sleeping pill before I leave, I stay on his good-girl list, and sometimes he even calls me afterwards and leaves messages on my machine.

"I'm sorry, Baby Girl, I don't remember anything that happened last night, we didn't go to bed, did we?"

And I call him back and reassure him, "No, everything's still the way you want it, pure."

Pure as coke, as the driven snow. I know all the dealers in town, they all hold meetings at Mark's place, the English guy with the crooked tie who swings golf clubs at me and says over and over, "You sod, you sod," and takes out little green scales to weigh my purchase; the Japanese guy in his designer sweaters with the yellow pills ten times as strong as morphine who watches me and waits for me to come down and call him, with his mercenary eyes and his Jag always parked just around the corner. They all have my number.

But then I have theirs. The old guy's the best. When I say around midnight, as I always do, that I have to leave, he tugs at me with his little white claw and says "No, please stay, please. I'll give you another two hundred, will you stay?" And then before his lip can curl back on itself, before he gets reflective and serious and says, "This is sad, isn't it, when you think about it, it's sad me calling you down here and paying you to listen to me," I run into the other room and find his checkbook. Some nights I have to fill it out for him; he puts it down and looks at me with deer eyes and that wan smile and says "I can't, I'm too drunk," and I fill it out and then guide his hand to the place where he has to sign, crookedly. And I take the check, plus the stash of twenty-dollar bills he's lined up for me on the kitchen counter on my way out. And give a little cheer as I run past the gardens and through the three gates to the marble elevator, because I've done it again, I'm still his Baby Girl.

So it doesn't matter about the back room, though yes, I have what one could call expenses. And a Baby Girl name, like Jane's, that will follow me pathetically from birthday to birthday. I never wanted to get older like ordinary teenagers, I knew there was nothing up there to look forward to except smelly old regulars and a parade of new girls, sixteen, seventeen, coming in illegally through the doors of every massage parlor in town and crowding me out. Days of humiliation, sitting in the back room sifting through an old Vogue, answering the phone, accompanying the girls to the vault where they drop half their money. Watching with a tired smile like the one Jane has on her lips these days, fussing with the ribbon in her hair, her tummy starting to round out under the tight white dress. They're my only family, Mario and the changing girls' faces, and the johns who ring the doorbell and grope at my stockings in the rooms upstairs where I go with a kit of condoms and jelly and baby powder, and a porn video to excite them into spending the fifty-dollar bills in their wallets if my naked body isn't enough.

Carol's ready, she's got on her high heels and she's waiting, nervous, beside me on the sofa. She doesn't have to say anything for me to know she's only done it a few times.

"Like, I'm not really sure about this," she whispers, plucking at her skirt. "Mark told me this guy is really nice, some Chinese guy, but, like, do I kiss him? Are you supposed to kiss them?"

"Well, I do," I say. "If you want to be special, you do too, because most girls won't," but by this time Mark's come out of his stupor on his end of the couch, and this Chinese guy is coming down the hallway with a big moon face.

Mark says, "This is Carol . . ." and Carol's face dims, and next thing I know she's in the kitchen, dragging Mark, and I can hear her saying, "Please, I need a fix before I go into the bedroom, please, Mark, don't do this to me, I thought you were my friend. I feel like you don't care, you won't listen to me, I don't even know this guy, just give me one fix before I go in."

And him saying "No, come on, Carol, don't be stupid, he'll know you're stoned, he says he only likes clean girls, girls who've never done drugs."

And I'm left alone with this guy in the living room. He stands there. I smile sweetly at him.

"You want a seat?"

"No, no, I'm sitting all day. In the office." He keeps standing there, toying with something in his jacket pocket, looking around with his lids lowered. He gives me a swift look, I cross my legs.

"Are you clean?" he says.

"Oh, sure," I say, keeping up that smile. "I never touch drugs, I don't even smoke."

It's true, that last bit, I quit a year ago.

"Good, you sound like a nice girl." He can hear Carol's voice from the kitchen, and he turns to me and says, "What about you, are you . . . ?" His voice is hesitant, the kind I like, the kind I can use. "I'll pay one hundred . . ."

"No," I say, laughing. I've worked hard all week, I'm loaded. "No, sweetheart, I'm on vacation. But Carol will do you."

I can hear Mark pushing her into the bathroom, giving up, and the john and I wait in the living room, him standing silently beside me, too nervous to fidget, and me swallowing the taste of chemicals and grinning into the middle distance until Carol comes out, her face shining, her eyes like disco balls, silver and spinning. She grabs me and whispers that she needs a condom, then disappears with the john into the bedroom, and Mark is waving a come-hither needle at me from the bathroom doorway.

It seems like days later that Carol emerges from the bedroom and I catch a rear view of the Chinese guy as he pads naked into the bathroom, but it can't be that long because she's only just coming down off the fix that Mark gave her.

"So, how'd it go?" I ask her, the way Jane asked me my first day at the massage parlor, when I came back from my first customer, holding a sealed envelope for the vault for Mario. "Was he okay?"

I don't remember how I answered, that first time, but Carol says nothing. Her eyes are muddy and they glance off me like it hurts to look straight at me, and she crosses the hardwood floor and steps out on the balcony. The sun is starting to come out, I can see the lemon light mixed with pink and blue around the edges of the curtains, I hear Mark in the bedroom getting comfortable on the bed that's just been vacated.

"Carol?" I say, but I can just make her out on the balcony, fumbling for a smoke, and I sink back into the cushions and pick up the needle she had left for me on the coffee table. And she stays out there like that for a long time, still and gray against the railings, and I know for a fact it's not because she likes sunrises.

THE SESSION

After she hung up the phone, Mary went to her closet humming. Later her boyfriend would be coming over, and for him she would wear lingerie and a floral perfume. She pushed the weighted hangers out of the way, reaching for the outfit pressed against the wall behind a row of sweaters and blazers. She drew it out shining, lay its slick black length across her bed as she began to undress. When her boyfriend arrived she would light the candles on her dresser, pour the wine into crystal glasses, she would undress him with the slow, savoring motions of someone unwrapping a beautifully packaged and long-awaited gift. She would kneel in front of him while he closed his eyes and stroked her hair. When he sighed and opened his eyes again, pulling his body away from her and reaching for his clothes, she would understand and not ask him to stay this time.

She pulled in her stomach and zipped up the black leather outfit, the studs outlining her breasts glinting like bullets in the mirror across the room. She slid her feet into her highest pair of heels and, four inches taller, tottered into the living room, where she scanned her collection of CDs. Opera, classical — those tragic, ethereal voices and instruments would be for later. Wine was cooling in the fridge, there were fresh flowers on the kitchen table, and she had vacuumed and tidied the apartment earlier in hopes that she would see her boyfriend tonight. Everything would be ready by the time she returned; now she had to hurry to get in the right mood for the session across town, or she would be late.

Rock music thudded through the apartment as Mary leaned into the mirror above the bathroom sink, painting on the face that would make her ready.

A cockatiel flew into the dining room and stood on the curtain rod above the window facing out onto the alley. It had a round spot of color on each cheek, like a circle of rouge or the center of a Japanese flag. Mary, distracted by its noisy flight, got up from the couch to have a closer look.

"Sshh," the man said from behind her as her heels clicked on the hardwood floor. She stopped obediently and lifted each leg with exaggerated care, glancing to her left at the locked bedroom door. The man's mother, an invalid, was sleeping behind it.

In the dining area, the cockatiel stared away from Mary, one bright eye fixed on the opposite wall.

"It's beautiful," she said, charmed by its indifference towards her.

"When I turn the lamp on, sometimes it comes in here," he said from the living room. Behind her a switch flicked and there was sudden brightness. She wanted to stay in the pink dining room, where halos of light were cast on the ceiling from upright lamps. The pink calmed her; it had the radiant, spreading effect of a sunset. She stood observing the cockatiel, which, without warning, flapped back into the kitchen and the further recesses of the house, shunning the light.

She returned to the living room, where the man was waiting. "You said you saw Mistress S. a few months ago. What was she like?"

"She's — well, she's good. There's not much to say, really. She's a grandmother, did you know that?"

"A grandmother?" Mary laughed in disbelief. "I knew she had kids, but . . ."

"A young grandmother, of course. She's in her early forties."

"I heard she's very good, very highly trained. She sent me over last night to one of her clients, as a kind of thank-you gift for some favors he had done for her. I've never met her, but she sounds interesting."

"Let's not talk about her, let's talk about you. You're beautiful. Thank you for coming here, for making yourself so beautiful for me." He looked at the glass in her hand. "How's your wine?"

Mary finished it in a gulp. She took a breath, and when she next spoke her voice was harsh. "Get me some more. And bring it to me on your knees."

"Yes, of course. I'll do anything for you." The man extracted the stem of the glass gently from her fingers. She stretched out on the couch with a half-smile on her lips, reaching up to tighten the leather strings fastening a spiked collar to her neck. It occurred to her that her boyfriend might not recognize her if he saw her now. She took another deep breath and began pressing her fingertips against the sharpened points of the spikes, unaware of the increasing pain. The collar framed her face, which was white with makeup. Her fingers were flecked with blood by the time the man returned, dropping to his knees at the entrance to the living room and holding the glass of wine like a chalice as he shuffled towards her.

She could not thank him. He dropped his head and kissed her black stiletto shoes. She reached out with one hand to stroke his hair, but withdrew it quickly when she felt the grease on her palm.

"Lick my shoes," she said. "Tell me how good they taste."

He moaned. "Oh, yes, they taste wonderful." He looked up at her with eyes as gray as mist, the depths turbulent and disturbed. They fixed on her face before he dropped them modestly and began to lap the bottoms of her shoes, taking a heel into his mouth and sucking. "Oh, thank you for letting me clean your shoes. You will let me do more, won't you? You'll treat me like . . . like white trash, won't you? You'll spit on me and treat me like garbage?"

She took this as a cue and gathered up the saliva into her mouth. He was staring at her with his churning eyes. She leaned forward and spat as hard as she could, flinging the spittle from her lips, but it landed somewhere below his neck. She tried again and again until it ran down his eyelids onto his cheeks, until he was licking it from the corners of his mouth.

"Oh, thank you," he murmured.

"You're garbage," she said. "White trash. You're scum!"

"Sshh," he reminded her, with a nod at the bedroom. She dropped her voice: "Scum. Let me spank you."

The man got up on his knees and pulled down his pants, which were stained at the crotch and sagged badly in the seat. "Do you want me to take my shorts off too?"

"No," she said hurriedly, holding her breath as the air filled with his smell. He stretched himself across her lap and she gingerly took the waistband of his shorts between her fingers and peeled them back.

"Thank me for hurting you," she said, as her hand cracked down.

"Thank you."

"Say, 'Thank you, Mistress, for hurting me.'"

"Oh, thank you, Mistress. Thank you for hurting me."

"How does that feel?" Her hand stung.

"It feels great. It feels great, Mistress."

She reached up to remove the spiked collar around her neck. Grasping it by the thongs, she smacked it across his buttocks, watching carefully. He made no sound of pain as beads of blood rose to the surface from the points of the spikes slapping into his flesh. He was patterned with red beads within seconds; she passed her hand over his rear in the semi-darkness of the living room, and his blood smeared across her palm. She laid her hand gently on him, smoothing the blood away, then drew the collar back around her neck.

He stood up, fastening his pants around his waist while another whiff of odor billowed out. His face was expressionless but the pupils of his eyes seemed to tumble around randomly, darkly.

"How do you feel?"

"I feel great, Mistress. Thank you." He dropped to his knees and pressed his lips to her feet, her calves, her knees. Impertinently, he reached up to kiss her cheek and she slapped him.

"Mmm, Mistress. You have such a beautiful face. I want to worship your body, I want to get wired on your body." His hands felt her calves, her arms. "You have such a strong and beautiful body." The back of his hand grazed her breast.

"You'll be punished for that. Crawl into the kitchen, and bring back something I can put inside you. Remember, you're my slave." She reached out and tenderly stroked a finger down his cheek. He looked at her. She drew back her hand and slapped him again.

"Yes, I'm your slave." He headed for the kitchen on his knees and she stood up from the couch, smoothing her skirt. In the mirror above the mantelpiece her face was flushed, her lips blood red above the spikes around her neck.

The carrot broke after a few thrusts, but the handle of the wooden spoon disappeared into him. She felt him clench around it, felt the grain of the wood grate against him. His eyes seemed to clench too. After a while he became open and depthless, and she was able to slide most of the bowl of the spoon inside him as well. She slid it in and out rhythmically and he received it with the moans of a woman.

When he came it was with a shudder that made his fat thighs tremble. Instinctively she moved away from him, worried that he might forget himself and clasp her to him in gratitude or passion. But after a moment of stillness, during which he looked down at himself with something like puzzlement, he got up and padded to the bathroom.

Later they sat beside each other on the couch and he told her that he loved her. It meant nothing to her, coming from him, though for an instant she felt a stab of pain — her boyfriend had never said he loved her. "I will do anything for you, you know that. Anything at all."

"I want to be the only dominatrix you see, the only woman you see. Do you understand that? If you say you'll do anything for me, you'll do that. You'll take me shopping, buy me leather and lingerie, and you won't see anyone else."

"I won't see anyone else, Mistress, just you. I'm so glad I found you."

"Let's dance," she said. The songs on the radio were all good, and she watched their reflections in the mirror. She could no longer smell him. She let his thick arms hold her close, and she teased him with the motions of her body. His face was a mask of pleasure and yearning. She kept glancing at the bedroom door, which hid the bedridden seventy-five-year-old woman from view. She wondered if the mother had heard the punishments inflicted on her son, and if these sounds would fill her dreams that night.

"Oh, Mistress," he said, and she let him bury his face in her neck while they circled around and around between the mirror and the locked door. She had to point to the time on the clock by the couch, adding that he would have to give her more money if he wanted her to stay longer, before he would let her go.

When the cab arrived, Mary had to take off her shoes to make her way down the icy stairs. When she turned to wave he blew her a sloppy kiss and did not close the door until the driver rounded the corner. Then he whirled around and around by himself in the living room to the silence of the old lady behind the locked door. The cockatiel, motionless on the curtain rod, continued to stare at the opposite pink wall. Its crest stood up, bristling, like an exclamation of its dignity.

After she got home she ran to the bathroom eagerly, removed her makeup and put on a white lace teddy with a pink ribbon tied between her breasts. An hour passed, and still her boyfriend did not appear to put his mouth over hers. She tried calling him, but could get nothing except his answering machine. After the twentieth or thirtieth attempt, someone picked up the phone but did not say hello. She listened to the fullness of the silence and was the first to put down the receiver. A moment later her phone rang, and when she picked it up it was her boyfriend's wife.

"Fuck off," she said. Then she hung up.

Mary stood there listening to the sound of the dial tone, absently wrapping the cord around and around her wrist like jewelry. After a while she unwrapped the cord and lay on her bed, cradling the receiver to her chest, pushing it down the lacy length of her body. Then her legs opened and she wept.

ROSES

The psychiatrist came into my life one month after my eighteenth birthday. He came into my life wearing a silk tie, his dark eyes half-obscured by lines and wrinkles. He brought with him a pronounced upper-class accent, a futile sense of humor, books to educate me. *Lolita. The Story of O.* His lips were thin, but when I took them between my own they plumped out and filled my mouth with sweet foreign tastes.

He worshiped me at first because he could not touch me. And then he worshiped me because he could only touch me if he paid to do so. I understood that without the autumn leaves, the browns of the hundreds and the fiery scarlets of the fifties, the marble pedestal beneath me would begin to erode.

The first two weeks were tender. He said he adored my childlike body, my unpainted face, my long straight hair. He promised to take care of me, love me unconditionally. He would be my father, friend, lover — and if one was ever absent, the other two were large enough on their own to fill up the space that was left behind.

He brought into my doorway the slippery clean smell of rain, and he possessed the necessary implements — samples of pills tiny as seeds, a gold shovel. My body yielded to the scrapings of his hands.

He gave me drugs because, he said, he loved me. He brought the tablets from his office, rattling in plastic bottles stuffed to the brim with cotton. I placed them under my tongue and sucked up their saccharine sweetness, learning that only the strong ones tasted like candy, the rest were chalky or bitter. He loved me beyond morality.

The plants that he brought each time he came to visit — baby's breath, dieffenbachia, jade — began to die as soon as they crossed the threshold of my home. After twenty-four hours the leaves would crinkle into tight dark snarls stooping towards the soil. They could not be pried open, though I watered his plants, exposed them to sunlight, trimmed them. It was as if by contact with him or with my environment, they had been poisoned. Watching them die, I was reminded of how he told me that when he first came to Canada he worked for two years in one of our worst mental institutions. I walked by the building once at night, creeping as far as I dared up the grassy slopes and between the evergreens. It was a sturdy beige structure, it didn't look so bad from the outside. In my mind, though, I saw it as something else. In my mind it was a series of black-and-white film stills; a face staring out from behind a barred window. The face belonged to a woman with tangled hair, wearing a nightgown. I covered my ears from her screams. When he told me about this place I imagined him in the film, the woman clawing at him where the corridors were gray, and there was the clanking sound of tin and metal. I used to lie awake as a child on the nights my father visited my bed and imagine scenes in which he was terrorized, in pain, made helpless. This was the same. I could smell the bloodstains the janitors had not yet scrubbed from the floors. I could smell the human discharges and see the hands that groped at him as he walked past each cell, each room. The hands flapped disembodied in the air, white and supplicating and at the same time evil.

He told me that when he was married to his first wife, she had gone shopping one day and he had had to take their baby with him on his hospital rounds. "I didn't know where to put him when I arrived," he said. "So I put him in the wastepaper basket." When he returned the child had upended the basket and crawled out, crying, glaring at his father. "I had no other choice," he said, and he reached into his trenchcoat and gave me a bottle of pills. "I love you," he said, "that's why I'm doing this."

I believed that only someone with a limitless love would put his baby in a trash can, its face squinched and its mouth pursing open in a squawk of dismay. Only someone like that could leave it swaddled in crumpled scraps of paper so he could go and take care of his patients. I could not imagine the breadth of the love that lay behind his eyes, those eyes that became as clear as glass at the moment of orgasm.

He bought a mask yesterday from a Japanese import store. It had tangled human hair that he washed with an anti-dandruff shampoo, carefully brushing it afterwards so the strands would not snap off. It had no pupils; the corneas were circles of bone. He took it home with him and stared at it for half an hour during a thunderstorm, paralyzed with fear. It stared back at him. It was supposed to scare off his rage, he said.

After two weeks his tenderness went the way of his plants — crisp, shriveled, closed. He stopped touching me in bed but grew as gluttonous as dry soil. I started to keep my eyes open when we kissed and to squeeze them shut all the other times, the many times he pulled my hand or my head down between his legs.

He continued to bring me magazines and books, but they were eclipsed by the part of him he expected me to touch. Some days, I found I could not. I thought it was enough that I listened to his stories. I fantasized about being his psychoanalyst and not letting him see my face, having that kind of control over him. I would lay him down on my couch and shine light into his eyes while I remained in shadow where he could not touch me.

His latest gift, a snake plant, looks like a cluster of green knives or spears. The soil is so parched that I keep watering it, but the water runs smartly through the pot without, it seems, having left anything of itself behind. The water runs all over the table and into my hands.

Tonight I did not think I could touch him. I asked him to hit me instead, thinking his slim white body would recoil from the thought. Instead he rubbed himself against my thigh, excited. I told him pain did not arouse me, but it was too late. I pulled the blankets around my naked body and tried to close up inside the way a flower wraps itself in the safety of its petals when night falls.

At first he stretched me across his knees and began to spank me. I wiggled obediently and raised my bottom high into the air, the way my father used to like to see me do. Then he moved up to rain blows upon my back. One of them was so painful that I saw colors even with my eyes open; it showered through my body like fireworks. It was like watching a sunset and feeling a pain in your chest at its wrenching beauty, the kind of pain that makes you gasp.

How loud the slaps grew in the small space of my apartment — like the sound of thunder. I wondered if my face looked, in that moment, like his Japanese mask.

The pain cleansed my mind until it breathed like the streets of a city after a good and bright rain. It washed away the dirt inside me. I could see the gutters open up to swallow the candy wrappers, newspaper pages, cigarette butts borne along on its massive tide. I saw as I had not seen before every bump and indentation on the wall beside my bed.

And then he wanted more and I fought him, dimly surprised that he wasn't stronger. I saw as though through the eye of a camera this tangle of white thighs and arms and the crook of a shoulder, the slope of a back. I scraped his skin with my fingernails. I felt no conscious fear because I was the girl behind the camera, zooming in for a close-up, a tight shot, an interesting angle. Limbs like marble on the tousled bed. His face contorted with strain. He was breathing heavily, but I, I was not breathing at all. I knew that if I touched his hair my hand would come away wet, not with the pleasant sweat of sexual exertion, but with something different. Something that would smell like a hospital, a hospital without disinfectant to mask the smells underneath.

And when he pushed my face against his thigh, it was oddly comforting, though it was the same thigh that belonged to the body that was reaching out to hit me. I breathed in the soft, soapy smell of his skin as his hand stung my back — the same hand that comforted crying patients, that wrote notes on their therapeutic progress, that had shaken with shyness when it first touched me. The sound of the slaps was amplified in the candlelit room. Nothing had ever sounded so loud, so singular in its purpose. I had never felt so far away from myself, not even with his pills.

I am far away and his thigh is sandy as a beach against my cheek. The sounds melt like gold, like slow Sunday afternoons. I think of cats and the baby grand piano in the foyer of my father's house. I think of the rain that gushes down the drainpipes outside my father's bathroom late at night when things begin to happen. I think of the queerly elegant black notes on sheets of piano music. The light is flooding generously through the windows and I am a little girl with a pink ribbon in my hair and a ruffled dress.

I seat myself on the piano bench and begin to play, my fingertips softening to the long ivory, the shorter ebony keys. I look down at my feet and see them bound in pink ballerina slippers, pressing intermittently on the pedals. Always Daddy's girl, I perform according to his instruction.

When it was over he stroked the fear that bathed my hands in cold sweat. He said that when we fought my face had filled with hatred and a dead coldness. He said that he had cured himself of his obsession with me during the beating, he had stripped me of my mystery. Slapped me human. He said my fear had turned him on. He was thirsty for the sweat that dampened my palms and willing to do anything to elicit more of that moisture so he could lick it and quench his tongue's thirst.

I understood that when I did not bleed at the first blow, his love turned into hatred. I saw that if I was indeed precious and fragile I would have broken, I would have burst open like a thin shell and discharged the rich sweet stain of roses.

Before he left he pressed his lips to mine. His eyes were open when he said that if I told anyone, he would have no other choice but to kill me.

Now that he is gone, I look between my breasts and see another flower growing: a rash of raspberry dots, like seeds. I wonder if this is how fear discharges itself when we leave our bodies in moments of pain.

The psychiatrist, when he first came, promised me a rose garden and in the mirror tomorrow morning I will see the results for the first time on my own body. I will tend his bouquets before he comes again, his eyes misty with fear and lust. Then I will listen to the liquid notes that are pleasing in the sunlit foyer and smile because somewhere, off in the distance, my father is clapping.

PLEASURE

The blindfold hugged her cheekbones. The window was open, the night air blew across her body. She licked her lips, tasting scotch and her own lipstick, the flavor of raspberries. She couldn't tell if it was raining or not; it sounded like rain outside, but sometimes traffic could sound like rain. She wasn't sure. She felt confused, cold without her clothes, and the skin itched where her hair brushed against her shoulderblades. She flexed the muscles in her face, trying to shift the blindfold, to let in some thin horizon of light.

But everything was dark.

A breeze blew over her breasts, her stomach. She shivered when his fingers closed on her wrist, tracing lightly the veins in her forearm. She started breathing hard when he took her arm and did that, running his thumb along the artery like it was a blade he was testing. For a wild moment she thought of bolting while she still could, but forced herself to lie still as he caressed her. She had made her decision by coming tonight, understanding fully what would happen to her if she did. Not like the first time, when she could not have known, when she had woken up the next morning in her own bed, drawn back the duvet, and seen what he had done to her body — this man who had touched the back of her hand so gently the night before when they met in the hotel lounge high above the city. "How sad you look," he had said. "Do you feel like talking?" She would have brushed him off if he had not said that he had once worked as a counsellor; although she had not been in therapy since the break-up of her marriage years ago, she automatically trusted people in the helping professions, saw them as full of wisdom and good intention. Green candles had flickered on the tables and he had let her drink and talk and even cry about the pressures of her job and the hopelessness of her ongoing affair with a married man. "What's that?" he had said then, grinning at her as she sniffed and wiped her eyes, "Is that a smile? Oh, I think so — right there, look, almost a smile, a little more, perfect!" And as they left for his apartment she had smiled dazzlingly through her tears.

The next morning she had spent wrapped in her sweater, slumped on her living-room floor in front of the fireplace, in shock. But underneath there had even then pulsed a vein of excitement, remembering the flames reflected in the stranger's green irises across the table, his oddly full, sensuous mouth. Remembering how at the instant she knew she was incapable of movement in his restraints, she had been stunned by how safe she felt in the absolute darkness of her life given over to another.

Now he pulled her left arm back past her head, buckling a strap of leather around her wrist. She wrapped her fingers around the bedpost, felt the leather clamping on her other wrist. A momentary silence. Where was he? Standing above her? Was he waiting by the far wall with lamplight on his face, studying her? She tried to turn her wrists but they would not turn inside the restraints.

Hands gripped her ankles, pulled them down. The slap of leather cuffs against bone, her legs stretched wide. Someone was breathing evenly in the room. She tried to move her limbs and couldn't. When she turned her head towards her right wrist, pulling at the shoulder, she could feel the tension all the way down her left leg to where her ankle was strapped to the railing. She was spread like a star on the bed, the cool comforter under her and the wind flying across her body.

Even as the fear increased, she felt a strange relief creeping in, that he was now in control of what would happen to her. She could not be held responsible for anything that happened next.

She thrust her hips towards the ceiling, pressing her fingers together and trying to slide them back through the cuffs.

She knew he liked to see her struggle. He was standing over her, breathing into her hair; she could feel his breath quicken with excitement, warmer than the air from the window. He tugged gently at her chin and then shoved a ball gag into her mouth, like a fist. She choked, panicked, forced herself to relax the muscles of her face. Leather straps ran down her chin and up her forehead; he lifted her head and started to buckle the straps underneath her hair. Pain clenched the base of her jaw as she held the ball between her teeth.

Someone crying, salt in her mouth and the fabric of the blindfold moist and hot. Something rising from her chest and her shoulders like an ache, something being massaged out of her until gradually a part of her mind grew dark and sleepy, cradled like a baby inside the restraints. A chain was dragged across her stomach, and then she felt the clamps bite into both nipples. He tugged at the chain, it lifted from her body in a silver arc, and her nipples rose to meet his invisible hands. Someone was still crying. Shut up, shut up, she wanted to say, but the sobs kept coming and wouldn't stop, like the first night in the lounge, when she wept in front of this stranger and felt the tremendous release. Then she heard the short, sudden whistling high in the air. It seemed to swoop down from the ceiling, and it split across the surface of her body.

Afterwards he sat by the bay window in his armchair, crossing his legs, adjusting the belt of his bathrobe. Light from the street lamps draped thin shadows over the floor, long and blue. He watched her across the room — she was bent over the bed, running her hands through her hair and then through the ropes and chains on the rumpled sheets. Her navy blazer lay crooked across her shoulders and her face was a blur of wet color, the smudged mouth, the pastel eyelids, and the wavy mascara lines down her cheeks. He didn't think she even knew that she was crying.

The air from the open window was crisp against his bare legs. He flicked the belt of the bathrobe off his thigh and reached for his cigarettes. Watched her lean down to pick up her dress, a designer affair from an expensive boutique; his eyes traced the buttons of her spine, her thin back. Women like her always did amaze him. Often they were as trusting as the underage girls he sometimes picked up in east-end bars with pool tables and staggering men in stained jeans and baseball caps. The only difference was that the girls grabbed their purses and ran from his apartment counting their blessings that they were still alive. The women with the careers and the condominiums were the ones who came back.

Now her hands were trembling, breasts bobbing inside the jacket like bruised fruit. He eyed her marks keenly: the welts, the drying blood zigzagging down her thigh, the abused nipples misshapen from the clamps that had remained on her throughout the session. Her breath was ragged in the air, halting like she'd forgotten how to breathe, then starting up again too fast, her throat chiseling up and down in her neck. He surveyed her body, then swiveled around to face the window.

It had begun to rain, lightly at first, and then coming down hard. Rain so thick it looked white in the night, smacking the pavement and the grass like bullets. Behind his own reflection in the windowpane he saw her straighten up, hiccupping, pushing hair out of her eyes and trying to fasten it in a clip at the base of her neck. The window reflected the lights of the chandelier blazing above the bed, the pink cloud of the comforter, the dull antique bed frame. The ropes lay uncoiled around her and the riding crop was propped against the wall, stiff and slender. He thought with pleasure that he could see its leather tongue still vibrating.

The rain poured down. He waited, and a moment of lightning filled the sky, bleaching everything silver — cars parked along the street, trees, other buildings. His own face loomed in the window, the smooth cheeks flushed boyishly from exertion, his lips curved and generous and undistorted by cruelty.

He rubbed his palm absent-mindedly. It was reddened from the friction of the whip handles. He glanced again at her reflection; she was sucking in her breath, trying to stop a sob. They both waited for the sound of thunder, but it came from so far away it could have been the sound of someone coughing in the next room of the west-end building.

He sighed, crushing out his cigarette and rising from the chair. Tonight he would let her go, and another night she would return. He knew. Already in the window he could see her starting towards him, tugging her skirt over her lashed thighs, as though he had done nothing.

MARRIAGE

His gold wedding band catches the light between the two walls of flesh that are our bodies in bed. It is a wide band with a perforated design, and it fits loosely on his finger. When he draws his hand up between us to touch me, the hand seems to take on a separate entity — as though it is a stranger's hand encountered in a crowded bus or an empty alley, the ring as hard as a weapon. I feel the coldness of it branding my skin. Yet I am drawn to it compulsively, this symbol of his commitment to another, as though it is a private part of him that will derive pleasure from my touch: rubbing it, twisting it, pulling it up to his knuckle and back down again.

In the morning we go for a walk in Queen Elizabeth Park, where a wedding is taking place. There are photographers bent on one knee in the grass, children with flowers looped through their hair, a bride in her layers of misty white. We watch from a bridge over a creek nearby, and then from the top of a waterfall. From that height the members of the wedding appear toy-like, diminished by the vast green slopes, the overflowing flower beds. When I glance sideways, I see him serenely observing the activity below, his hands draped over the low rail. I want then to step behind him, put my hands between his shoulders, and push him over, if only to recognize something in his face, some anxiety or pain to correspond with what I am feeling.

The people we pass in the park see a middle-aged man in a suit with his arm around a nineteen-year-old girl. They invariably pause, look twice with curiosity. At first I look back boldly, meeting their eyes in the harsh sunlight, but as the walk wears on my gaze falters. I keep my eyes trained on the ground, my pointy white high heels keeping step with his freshly polished black leather shoes. I don't know what people are thinking; I know they don't think I am his daughter. Their stares make me feel unclean, as if there is something illicit about me. Suddenly I wonder if my skirt is too short, my lipstick too red, my hair too teased. I concentrate hard on pretending that there is something natural about my odd pairing with this man.

He is oblivious to their looks; if anything, he is pleased by them, as though people are looking because the girl his arm holds captive is particularly striking. He does not see that the looks are more often edged with pity than any degree of approval or jealousy.

He tells me afterwards that he is proud to be seen with me.

Sometimes when he visits me he is carrying his beeper. He has just completed the crawl to the foot of my bed, drawn up the comforter tent-like over his head and shoulders, and is preparing in the fuzzy dark to attack my body with his tongue. And then from deep in the gray huddle of his pants on the floor rises the berating call of the beeper, causing the anonymous bulk under the covers to jump and hit his head against the soft ceiling of the comforter. I resist the urge to reach out and rub that dome under my comforter, like it is a teddy bear or my own bunched-up knees.

Naked, he digs into the mass of material on the floor, extracts the beeper, and seats himself on the edge of the bed. I tuck my hair behind my ear and examine his back as he dials a series of numbers to access his answering service, the hospital, other doctors.

"Good afternoon," he says. "Is this Dr. Martin? Yes . . . yes . . . how is she? All right, one milligram lorazepam to be administered at bedtime . . ." while he remains half-erect between his long white thighs, one hand groping behind him 'til it finds and begins to squeeze my breast and then its nipple. Even though he has tucked the phone between his ear and shoulder so that the hand that flaps the air is not the one that wears the ring, I still feel it belongs to someone other than him as it rounds the blank canvas of his back and pats air and pillow before touching skin. I am reminded of the card in my desk drawer: on Valentine's Day four months ago he gave me a card that read, in a floral script, "I Love You." He said, almost immediately, "I hope you don't get vindictive and send that card to my wife. It's got my handwriting on it."

It never would have occurred to me to do so if he hadn't told me. What he said inspired me to keep the card in a special drawer, where I will not lose it. I put it away feeling reassured that at last I had some power over him. I had something I could hurt him with. I now know I saved the card because it was my only proof of his love for me, it is the only part of him that belongs to me.

The night before his wife's return from the conference she's attending in Los Angeles, we drive to our usual restaurant where the Japanese waiter smiles at us in a way he interprets as friendly, while I recognize amusement dancing at the corners of his mouth. I lift my purse into my lap and politely ask permission to smoke.

"I'd rather you didn't. My wife has a good nose for tobacco."

How much I want his wife to come home to the smell of smoke in the family car. After she has walked off the plane and through the terminal to where her luggage revolves on the carousel, after she has picked out his face among the faces of other husbands waiting to greet their wives and take them home, I can see her leaning back in the passenger seat, rubbing her neck, tired after her flight and eager for sleep — then the trace of smoke acrid in her nostrils, mingled perhaps with my perfume. In my fantasy she turns to him, wild-eyed and tearful, she demands that he stop the car, she wrenches the perforated wedding band from her finger and throws it at him before she opens the door and leaves. *Give it to that slut*, she will say.

"Maybe I'm subconsciously trying to ruin your marriage," I smile as I light a cigarette and watch the smoke momentarily fill up the front of the car

"Please don't," he says calmly. I think a man whose marriage is in my hands should sound a little more desperate, but in the dark I can only see his profile against the stores and buildings blurring outside the window, and it is unreadable. I wish afterwards that I had looked at his hands, to see if they tightened on the wheel.

He tells me that we will have lots of time together over the years but I have no concept of time. I ask him to leave the city with me.

"Would you really do that?" he asks. "Run off with me?"

"Yes."

"I'm very flattered."

"Don't be. It wasn't meant to be flattering." I pause. I want to say, *It meant more than that.* "Why can't we just take off?"

"I can't do it right now," he says. "I have people depending on me — my patients. I'd love to. I can't."

"I have just as much to lose as you do, you know," I say, but he doesn't believe me. He has been feeding me whisky all evening, and I am swaying in a chair in front of him. He places my hands together between his own and pulls me out of the chair, collapsing me to my knees. Kneeling, I sway back and forth and squint up at him, my hands stranded in his lap.

"You should go," I say.

"Yes, I have to work tomorrow morning."

"And you have to pick your wife up from the airport," I say, struggling to my feet to press the color of my lips against his white cheek.

I do not realize I am clutching the sleeve of his suit jacket until we have reached the door, where he chuckles and pries my fingers loose. He adjusts his beeper inside his pocket and walks out into the rain-misted night.

Back inside the apartment I am intent on finishing the bottle of Chivas he left behind on the kitchen counter, but when I go to it I find an envelope next to the bottle, weighted by an ashtray. I tear it open, my heart beating painfully — it could be a letter, he could be saying that he can no longer live without me, that tonight he will finally tell his wife about us. Instead I pull out a greeting card with a picture on the front of a girl standing by a seashore. She is bare-legged, with dimpled knees, wearing a loose frock the color of daffodils. She looks about twelve years old.

Inside are no words, just two new hundred-dollar bills.

He tries to alleviate his guilt by giving me money: checks left folded on the kitchen table, crisp bills tucked inside cards. He takes me shopping for groceries and clothes, he never visits my apartment without bringing me some small gift, as though all this entitles him to leave afterwards and return home to his wife. But I have no similar method of striking such bargains with my conscience. The dregs of our affair stick to my body like semen. Because I do think of his wife — of the way she must sink into bed beside him in the dark, putting her face against his chest and breathing him in, his scent carried with her into her dreams. I do think of the pain she would feel if she knew, and I am frightened sometimes by the force of my desire to inflict that pain upon her — this wife who is to be pitied in her faithless marriage, this wife whom I envy.

And tonight I want more than anything to take those smooth brown bills between my fingers and tear them up. Does he think I'm like one of those teen hookers in thigh-high boots and bustiers he says he used to pick up down-town before he met me? My hands are shaking, I want so badly to get rid of his money. Instead I go over to the chest of drawers beside my bed and add this latest contribution to the growing stack of cards and cash I have hidden there.

He often says to me, "If you were my daughter . . ." My lips twist and he has to add each time, "You know what I mean." If things were different, he means. If we weren't sleeping together. We cultivate fantasies for each other of what a loving, doting father he would have made me; of what a pretty, accomplished daughter I would have made him. "I adore you," he says to me. "I wish I could marry you." And then, "I wish you were my daughter," as he kisses my neck, my shoulders, my breasts, his fingers slipping between my thighs. As things are, I see we don't have anything that comes close to the illusion.

His cologne has found places to lodge in my blankets, clothing, cushions. No matter how many loads of laundry I carry down the back stairs, the smell of him has taken up residence in the corners of my apartment, as though to stay.

He tells me little about his activities, but the spare portraits he paints grow vivid in my mind. This weekend he will visit Vancouver Island with his family. I picture them on the ferry, with the possibility of gray skies and rain, the mountains concealed by veils of fog, the treed islands rising like the backs of beasts out of the ocean. I wonder if his family will venture onto the deck and look down at the water, I imagine them falling overboard and being ground to pieces by the propellers, staining those foamy waves crimson.

He's told me about his three sons and I know they are all teenagers. I know that the oldest is stronger than his father, handsome with a thick head of red hair, and that this son's feisty girlfriend reminds him of me. I know they tease him with the eyeball-rolling exasperation and embarrassment that I've felt towards my own parents.

"Oh, Dad," they'd groan in restaurants where he'd be teasing the waitress. "Don't *do* that. She's in our class at school!"

I imagine him clambering up the gray steel ladder leading to the top deck of the ferry. He reaches down towards his wife. When she grips his hand his ring bites into her palm, a sensation she has grown used to, as though the ring is now a part of his body.

They walk together behind their children, past rows of orange plastic chairs in the non-smoking section, past the cafeteria selling sticky danishes and styrofoam cups of hot coffee, past the gift shop with the little Canadian flags and sweatshirts in the window. They wrestle open the heavy door leading onto the deck and the blast of air sucking them out separates his hair into pieces plastering forward, backward, tight against his cheek.

His family races in their sneakers and jeans towards the edges of the ferry, clinging to the railings, and he fights his way through the wind towards them, laughing and shouting. I know for certain that, for once, he is not thinking of me.

GLASS

She has put her fist through the window of her apartment. As she pulls her arm back, along with half the window, the shards slice across her wrist and the palm of her hand, simple as a knife slicing through uncooked white chicken meat. The blood begins to fill the gash to the brim, spilling over, as she looks down at her hand with detachment. The sound of glass falling fills her ears with wind chimes, the sound of glass spinning in the blue night. Ballerinas of glass cling to her wrist; she plucks them out, lets them fall to the floor.

She walks to the bathroom and holds the cut hand under the tap, filling the sink with diluted blood. She smiles to herself — she always smiles when she feels broken and ground-up, with nothing left except a diamond in her chest. A diamond that nobody can pluck out and possess. A diamond beautiful like herself. She knows she is beautiful, because the sure, sharp mirror tells her so.

I see someone in the mirror, though, who is not beautiful, and that is why she hates me. I am the part of her she wants to kill. She has tried before, but what she doesn't know is that if it wasn't for me she would have died long ago. I won't let her die; even if she doesn't like me, I won't. Maybe that is why she hates me so much. I'm the one who holds her together, and how can I help it if I see bloodshot eyes and the pores of her skin when she bends over the mirror?

The blood mingles in the water in the sink, in sluggish streaks. The water becomes the color of roses. She can hear the glass falling in her apartment; her attention has always been held by bright and flashing things, and she is awed at having created the scattering glass with its private, special orchestra. She loves anything prismatic, fake or real. Chandelier droplets. Diamonds. Treasure buried in white lines. . . . She wraps her hand in a towel, watching the blue material become tie-dyed with splotches of red. She walks back to the living room and sees the window, an open mouth in the night, dripping glass.

I wish she would pick up the phone and call someone. I want to help her, but she will do whatever she wants to, as she always has. She needs stitches, but although the cut — so clean and deep — was painless, she is terrified of blind needles probing the depth of the wound. That she is never afraid of anything unusual, but will flee from the ordinary, is a remarkable contradiction. She is all contradictions, her need and her dependency warmly sloshing inside her, and on the surface the frozen lake for others to skate on. I know all this. I don't know why she can't hear my voice. I'm the only one who can love her unconditionally, but she persists in looking outwards.

She stands, holding her hand, near the waterfall of glass. She wants to be with someone brilliant and crazy and artistic like herself. As she thinks this, a smile leaps around her mouth and she spins, dodging the glass that flies into the room. It winks at her lethally from the carpet. She bends over and picks up a piece, stroking it carefully with her finger; it has a sharp, sexy, dangerous curve to it.

Do you see why I am worried about her? Her hand has stopped bleeding, but I don't like the way she acts in times like this, when the white lines seem to tighten their weave around her, when, with her eyes closed, she sees a razor busily cutting, chopping, dividing. But the lines are not the problem; the problem is that she is like a new-born baby who will die without touch. Only my arms can enfold her body, and sometimes, strangely, I want her all to myself. I want it to be just me and her, forever. Like diamonds. Forever. I could rescue her each time from her madness. I could catch the fragments of her and hold them together when she falls and cracks open. Whenever she spins like this, dizzily, I could press each star of her close and protect her.

She stands static, thinking of Allan as the flakes of glass hum in the background. The last time they had been together, she had lain there looking up at him with so much trust in her eyes. He had looked back down at her without smiling, without tenderness, in the 3:00 A.M. dimness. She had seen embarrassment and anger in his face as he thrust himself in and out of her deliberately, one of her white legs stretched up like an arching swan's neck onto his shoulder. Perhaps that trust had frozen him because he could not meet it. Perhaps he could not admire her for this. Perhaps he too only craved things beyond his reach and despised her for giving herself to him. But how else could she have done it? He never phoned, though from the first night he had said he loved her, would have married her if . . . if she wasn't so needy? If she didn't pull at him quite so much, trying to take hold of just a corner of him to pull down into her blackness? Allan called himself a marketer of mirages. His phone began ringing every morning at 5:00 with stock-market representatives from New York; he sauntered whistling to his sports car to drive to company meetings. On the evenings when he came to pick her up, jazz on the radio, the web of stars jailed her and she reeled, spinning apart from the speed. Those nights when he buried his head between her thighs for hours, arduous, relentless, she had always felt as if he was trying to take her to some place where she did not belong. Maybe he was searching for the diamond inside her? That was why although in her mind and behind her shut eyes she was looming larger and larger, threatening to branch out, transcend her body, she stayed intact, with her nails digging into the hands on her belly. Their nights grew progressively silent until they never talked anymore; he busily digging with his tongue, she fighting the commands of her body.

No, she could not whirl seductively on the edge of his world. I see that, I see how impossible it all was, and how she had to phone him then, late at night when the white lines had faded and she would speed in a dark cab across the city, looking at the lights colorful and cold. It disturbs me that she was always in such bad shape when she arrived, was always pulling and dragging at his corners. They could have loved each other, measured out equal amounts of light and dark for each other, if she hadn't been on the verge of what she thought was death. If maybe, just once, she had not called him and made herself ugly by whispering *I need you*. Because, though he is the one person who could live with her level of pain, he didn't choose to. I don't think he was contemptuous of her, exactly. It was only that once, just once, he would have liked to see her real smile, not the crazy butterflies that flitted around her mouth. He would have enjoyed that, I think. They could have built something together then, from that one smile.

But she stands now at the jaws of the window, her hand clothed in tie-dyed cotton, listening to the radiant music of falling glass. She pictures Allan in his penthouse bed, with the mountains melting outside the window, the city gathered together and pooled beneath the balcony. The wind is blowing into his apartment, over the crystal ball on his desk, over the bamboo plants, over the waterbed. He is settling under the rose-colored comforter, grateful for the silent phone, the stars floating past the breathing green bamboo, past the pulsating crystal, settling around the mountains.

She stands there, holding her own hand, empty of pain. She watches the glass swoop from the window onto the pavement below, sprawling like dancers in lewd but beautiful positions on the sidewalk. And I hold her hand and tell her that it is better this way, that I am the only one she has, the only one who can keep her safe. She nods, and the diamond glitters in a lump in her chest, intact, and I take her hand and guide her away from the music, down a line of soft white glass.

FETISH NIGHT

The club is black-painted, underground. Sabina hears the rattle of the chains before she reaches the end of the narrow corridor. The clunk of boot heels on the floor, the creak of tight leather pants. Justine walks slightly ahead, her body sharp and as purposeful as an arrow. When Justine's jacket swings open, Sabina sees her friend's familiar breasts exposed, the squarish nipples sticking out like antennae from her chest.

The bartender is naked, but his piercings give him the appearance of being dressed, thin crescents of gold and silver jutting from different points in his body. Justine orders soda, Sabina a vodka on ice. Together they make a quick tour of the club, squeezing between knots of people wearing smooth black leather or bare skin, many glittering with studs and rings. Several men have hoods fitted over their heads, resting like mantles on their shoulders. An Oriental woman stands against the wall, a latex sheath outlining her curves, plucking with a red fingernail at the juncture where stocking and garter belt meet. A blonde wearing a cocktail dress and a loop of gold and diamonds around her neck is being strapped stomach-down to a table, ropes and cuffs materializing to curl around her waist, wrists, ankles. A slave hangs his head by the doorway, a spattering of tiny bulbs blinking around his crotch, his girlfriend pressing the button in a small box tucked into the rear of his underwear.

Over by the piano, Sabina notices a man watching her steadily, with his hands clasped in front of him. He lowers his eyes when she returns the gaze but does not move otherwise, as though chained to the spot. She decides to ignore him for now, moving to the lounge area where there are paintings on the wall she can't quite make out in the dark, but they seem to be landscapes: men in bulky sweaters walking dogs near cliffs, waves crashing against rocks and spraying the sky. She chooses a plush, high-backed chair, and Justine clambers onto the arm, resting one foot on the seat and dangling the other leg. Stroking Sabina's hair with one hand, she points out the key players with her cigarette in the other — the internationally known male dom, the female pain freak who was runner-up in several tattoo contests, the trans-sexual centerfold model. In the dark the model's eyes are a wet washed-out blue, wide and heavily lashed above the cheekbones where the skin is stretched tight enough to break.

Sabina sets her drink on a wooden table beside her. The glass is sweating from the melting ice and the heat of the bodies in the room. The club is full, each person taking up extra space with the accoutrements they wear, the collars protruding with nails and screws, the paddles and whips hanging from belts looped around their hips. Across from her, two girls barely out of their teens are huddled together on a corner of a couch. One is wearing a headband which tugs all her hair off her forehead, making her appear even younger and more vulnerable. They say nothing to each other, but watch with the nervous, insatiable gaze of voyeurs. No one in the club approaches them.

The whipping has been going on for some time. A man is stretched out unrestrained on a table, gripping a piece of leather between his hands. He is naked except for underwear and a leather collar and bracelet. Another man, wearing a fluffy shoulder-length wig and lipstick, his body tightly laced in garter belt and a merry widow, is circling him expertly, flicking at his legs and the slope of his back with whips of various sizes. After half an hour of warm-up he is dancing around his lover, his arm rising and falling with tireless strength, blows hailing upon the man's body. As the flogging crescendoes, Justine scrambles closer to

Sabina until she is almost sitting on her lap, the soda forgotten in her hand. Sabina curls her arm under her friend's jacket and presses her breast comfortingly. The man on the table has already taken more pain than anyone she has seen, but it is a while yet before he begins to bite on the leather strap in his hands, like a woman giving birth. Shouts escape his lips, and he turns his face towards Sabina. His eyes are black and tortured and he is staring straight at her. It seems for a moment as if he is trying to draw strength from her face, which she keeps impassive. His eyes hold hers as his lover whips him with all the strength in his arm in the now utterly silent club, his eyes tell her not to blink or breathe, not to disturb the spell. Only when he ducks his head down again to clamp his teeth on the strap does Sabina's heart start beating again, hurtfully, as if she is being pounded repeatedly from inside her chest. The whipping must stop but it doesn't stop, the people standing around in their elaborate costumes no longer seem threatening, their chains hang limply by their chaps, one or two women are stepping forward to tell the man he is whipping the same spot repeatedly, he mustn't do that, he's hurting him too badly, and still the whip descends on breaking flesh and the walls and the ceiling are ringing with its sound. The man on the table is finally crying, his whole body rising and falling with his sobs as if his body was a white and pink wave of raw flesh.

Long after any tolerable ending, the beating stops. His wigged lover, breathing hard, tugs the strap tenderly out from between his fingers and helps him off the table. The man staggers and almost falls, and the two make their way supporting each other through the crowd. People clear a wide path for them, and the silence takes a long time to form again into conversation. People cough and clear their throats, testing their voices as if using them for the first time. In a corner, before they disappear through a doorway, the man in the wig kisses his bleeding lover, and Sabina hears for a moment their soft, commiserating laughter.

The man who has been watching Sabina all evening is suddenly, magically, on his hands and knees in front of her. She looks at Justine and shrugs; her friend grins and moves into another chair, tucking her knees up to her naked chest, drawing on her cigarette. The man kisses the floor around Sabina's feet, and when she crosses her legs he cautiously moves towards her dangling shoe. His face reminds her of a storm cloud — soft brown curls, bushy eyebrows, large turbulent eyes, and a bow mouth in a round face. Reaching between his legs her hand collides with the pendulum of his penis, cloaked in rich, supple leather. Without being asked, he draws a whip from the belt around his waist the way a soldier might unsheathe a sword, surrendering it to her, and she begins to step around him in the first stages of the tormentor's dance, the music familiar and dependable, the whack of leather against skin, the small unchecked cries of pain.

♦   ♦   ♦

Sabina's slave is circling the club now, as he has been ordered to do, his ass raised high and his forehead bent to the ground. He is alternately barking and howling. People make room for him, glancing at Sabina curiously, smiling now that the tension from the man's whipping on the table has been replaced by a more playful mood. A girl with cropped hair and rings piercing the skin of her temples, nose and neck asks to borrow the slave for a ride, and when Sabina assents she climbs nimbly onto his back and digs the heels of her ankle boots into his side, yipping, her small neat body arched in pleasure. Occasionally she reaches behind her to strike his rump with a leather strap. When the slave returns, head bent, to Sabina's side, the girl dismounts him and thanks her, returning him with a bow and a flourish of her hand.

Fetish Night is almost over. Lights blink on in different parts of the club, exposing white faces and garish makeup on the women and some of the men. Sabina heads for the bathroom, which is a modern, unfriendly cavern of mirrors and polished cement. She and Justine leave through lit passageways, brushing against the other club-goers who appear startled in their states of transition, many carrying changes of clothing draped in rustling bags over their arms.

♦   ♦   ♦

Outside, taxis line the block. People emerge from the change room at the rear of the club, unrecognizable in shirts and slacks, jeans, pantyhose and trench coats. The sky is lit by street lamps and a light, cold rain has begun to fall, sticking in the air like snow. Justine waves at a taxi, digging her other hand into her tight leather pants for warmth. Someone touches Sabina hesitantly on the arm and she turns to find her slave with his eyes lowered, handing her a folded piece of paper. She opens it to find his phone number, but when she turns to say good-bye he has already disappeared, down the block or into a cab, or back into the shadows between the broken, shuttered buildings in the neighborhood. As she slides into the waiting cab, Justine points out the man who had been whipped on the table. Sabina would not have known it was him, otherwise. He is fully dressed and walking with an easy, swinging gait down the street, his denim-clad, de-wigged lover beside him. As they round the corner she notices they are almost the same height, their shoulders bumping gently as they disappear from sight.

MERCY

It is your wife's fortieth birthday, and I am torturing you to the sounds of a tape of Dylan Thomas giving a poetry recital. His voice is theatrical, and at times it hovers at the edges of breaking into song. "Do not go gentle into that good night . . . Rage, rage against the dying of the light . . . ." His words, charged with command, seem to pulse through my own body. Obediently I slip the spiked heel of my shoe into your mouth. You are watching me with confusion because I am drunk and balancing over your naked body takes more skill than you think. I don't want to fall on you with my weight and the stabbing silver of my bracelet, injuring you, making it impossible for you to meet your wife later in the evening for dinner down by the harbor where the white ships come in. She will chatter on about

The New York Review of Books, literary magazines, publishers' conventions, and other things that bewilder you because you decided to make money in medicine instead of writing poetry. Neither of us knew when we made our respective choices that we might be equally unfulfilled. I do not want to hurt you, at least not clumsily, not out of drunkenness, not because the high arches of my feet prevent me from balancing in spike heels. I want it to mean something when I hurt you, I want each transgression to be a deliberate one that cuts both ways, something that neither of us will be able to blame on bottles of wine or the fact that when I am in this position, one foot balanced on your neck, there is nothing nearby to hold on to and the only thing stable is the floor which seems a long way off from up here.

I will not go gentle into you. The high heel of my shoe is in your mouth, and it is cutting the roof where the flesh is ridged and ticklish. You suck the heel as you would a phallus, and I wonder what you are tasting, what grotty remains of dust and dirt and sidewalk you are swallowing down the soft pinkness of your throat. Up here I can see you are going bald, the expanse of your forehead with your gray hair tossed backwards onto the carpet is wide and gleaming. With your eyes shut and your mouth working to please the point of my shoe, you could easily be an inflatable doll or a cartoon and I am able then to withdraw my heel as carefully as a penis and rake it in pink crescents across your cheek and down your chin.

In my sessions with you I search for the evil inside us that we share like kisses between our open mouths. The boundaries I once saw as steel fences in my mind turned out to be sodden wooden planks when I reached them, easily kicked down. Each act of pain became easier to inflict once the initial transgressions had been committed, and we had understood ourselves capable of surviving them. Once I even tried on myself the things I do to you. Whipping myself with a silver chain, I became fascinated by the stopped seconds of pain that opened my mouth and closed my eyes. Afterwards I was left looking down at my thighs where the circle of the chain I had snapped down my body had left a perfect imprint of itself, pink like a rubber stamp, like one of those playful rubber stamps with happy faces on them.

When the pain stopped, time moved again and I wondered if perhaps in our time together you felt this also, this stopping of time as it races past you now that you are middle-aged and some of your friends are already dead. Perhaps only the absorption of pain can distract you from the details of your daily life — the necessary hours at the office, the teenaged children demanding money for concerts and clothes, the golf lessons on weekend afternoons. All this leading you down the road of increasing age, minor illnesses, and death.

"Old age should burn and rave at close of day," Thomas instructs sternly. Perhaps only in the clutches of pain, when your eyes are closed and your lips forced apart, does the day seem long. Perhaps this is what you seek, this element of immortality, the way I do by writing poems. I tried that day to understand what it must be like for you when the pain hits, when you protest with a convulsion in your voice that stops me because it is no longer a pleasurable pleading that runs out of your mouth like water or thin blood.

It is easy to become addicted to hurting you, to aching for that moment when you take off your clothes and lie on my floor. There is a slight roundness to your stomach and a soft field of black chest hair that sharpens into a tiger's stripe running down your belly. It appears knife-like, sadistic. I could picture you with a black beard, trying on black leather vests and turning in a mirror like the men I watch downtown in the shops I frequent now, fascinated, struck by how warmly this fringe community welcomes me. I had never been accepted so unquestioningly elsewhere. I finger the bewildering chains of my new trade, and talk to the women behind the counter who are pierced and smiling and who recommend books that make me realize I am only on the circumference and that the center has no bottom. You could just as easily have been one of those men who advertise for young blonde slaves to torture, who read magazines that teach them how to build benches and restraints and instruments of pain. You could have turned out like that, and I am given to understand that perhaps even now, one afternoon you will. Some nights I pace my apartment and wonder if one day I will push you too far and you will lunge up from the floor and hurt me. There is no way either of us can tell, because we are each other and there is nothing restraining that moment when we exchange power as others do body fluids.

The power floods into me warm and soft and golden, dusty as pollen. I had not realized previously the extent of my emptiness that no kisses could fill, no flowers or brave words of love. The emptiness sang hollow and blue and then turned red as rage. I knew from the first session that I could have killed you, and that, indeed, you were not letting me go so far as I needed. Looking down at your muscled body on my floor, I wanted some of that red inside me to bleed out through you, in slashes and strokes of thudding color.

You bought me a bracelet the other day from one of the sex shops downtown. It was sitting curled up in a dusty corner of the glass case, half-concealed by wrinkly dildoes and packets of dayglo creams and lotions. I was browsing impatiently, needing to use the bathroom, my feet swelling in my heels, bored by the plastic-coated magazines and the multi-colored underwear nailed to the walls. The woman behind the counter had a toothless glazed expression and eyes that looked like they were made of glass. I did not particularly want to be there and perhaps neither did you, you were lifting your watch every so often to check the time and thinking of dinner with your wife who, if you were lucky, might wear the red leather outfit you had bought her, even if she never assumed the role. There was no time that afternoon to duck into changing rooms with burgundy lace and ripped, fringed leather skirts. The fluff no longer interested me, the delicacy of lingerie seemed an offence. It was the trickling cat o'nine tails that tickled my fingers, it was the canes perched rigid on the walls, it was even that morbid black leather mask molded to the dummy's unseeing white face on the top counter that ran currents through me. I felt as though the world I had walked on for years had flipped and on the other side there lived people who turned up palms of blood and leather.

The woman with the motionless eyes uncurled the bracelet and we felt the tips of the studs. When she said the bracelet had been banned I said I wanted it and you paid for it and that night I fell asleep with it on my wrist, while candles flickered around the room in crystal holders. It tormented me all night because each time I moved my hand I would hurt myself into consciousness. The next day I wore it and pretended it was a joke from a friend, and at lunch a man came to my table and said, "You could kill somebody with that." His eyes were brown and overly trusting. Later when I hugged my lunch companion good-bye she let out a yelp and said, "You stabbed me in the back."

It will be a good toy for next time, applied to the more vulnerable parts of your body. I will stroke you with the eager points of the bracelet and then I will hurt you with them. That is part of the joy, the caresses that I allow before pressing down the pain. I like it best when I kiss you with full-mouthed tenderness before slapping your face; when I lick a finger and circle it lightly around the head of your penis before pinching the skin of the shaft; when I take one of your truncated nipples into my mouth and stroke its little hard point between my teeth before I bite.

I listen to you when you call at night needing somebody to talk to, and I spend half an hour with you on the phone while you talk about your marriage and your kids and your practice, and I never tell you you are boring me or that my time is not for you. I show my harmlessness by giving you books of poetry, but I am never able to read more than a few lines aloud to you before you become impatient and pull me to the floor, where we lose our words and our regular faces.

If we are victims of each other, then in those moments we are the most beautiful victims in the world. Sometimes when I stand over you, when my heels are gouging into you, I look beyond you towards some thin line of distance and understand that each time your face wrenches with pain I am spreading a slow dark stain down the still-white years of my future, and that in that sense you are killing me and not the other way around. Each time you scream, it wrings out the light in me and leaves twisted red and black cords like knotted whips lying on the wall and waiting, hungering to be used, to be applied against white skin that flinches away and cries.

You have the kind of engaging smile and blue eyes that, in the daytime, makes you one of the most popular dentists in the city. How could they know those same fingers take a piece of wire and wind it so tightly around the base of your penis that I wince for you? How could they know your mouth fills with everything that sifts across the bottom of high-heeled shoes that have walked the pavement? You are friendly enough, your hand cups their trusting chins, you see into them and reassure them. You see into them the way you saw into me the first night we met over drinks and lounge music, and even though I said little and at that time knew nothing, you saw something in me you described as dark, very dark; you saw a part of me I had not seen in hours of mirror reflections.

This is not a game, you kept saying, until I heard it every night in my dreams. You can call it a game if you like, but I will do almost anything you want, whatever that might be.

I had thought that that for me would translate into walks on the beach and poetry readings and drinking wine, that those would be the extent of my desires. I had not expected this rage that continues to grow rather than subside as you plead with me now to stop, as a thin growl rises in my throat and razors the air.

It is your wife's fortieth birthday and Dylan Thomas's voice slows to a stop on the tape. You edge out the door with the sun bouncing off your glasses and your briefcase tucked under your arm. It is always remarkable to me, these partings, how we are able to assume again the responsibilities of work and life as though nothing had changed, as though we had not been permanently altered by our actions. On the surface things are as they always have been — you are discreet with your wounds; no one asks questions. I sit down at the typewriter and rub my swollen feet, their chafed heels, thinking of our obligations towards wives and poetry and thinking that perhaps this is just as well, we do not want the end to come too soon, the irreversible outcome of the final scene. We want to taste our pleasure bit by bit, inch by inch, we want to lick it slowly and make it last. We will make it good and make it last, my poor tiger-striped victim, we will make ourselves into people we hate enough to kill.

THE
APARTMENTS

The man's shower curtain is decorated with coral and fish. Jane is reminded of another apartment, the one where the diver lived. But she won't think about that. This is a different bathroom, with a *Playboy* smoothed under a travel magazine on the counter, a triangular bottle of cologne on a shelf, the absence of a medicine cabinet behind the mirror. And a scale on the floor, where the diver would have kept his masks, both the one he used underwater and the one he used in bed.

It'll be fine here. It'll be different from the other nights. This time, it'll be good. Jane peels up the edges of the travel magazine and takes a peek at the Playmate of the Month, blonde and for some reason wearing a crown. She lifts her eyes to the mirror and shrugs. This relaxes her shoulders, so she does it again. A strand of dark brown hair falls over her forehead, and she pushes it back with fingers that tremble in the critical light from the row of bulbs above the mirror. According to the reflection her face is bloated, her hair needs washing, and there are avocado-colored circles under her eyes. Plain Jane. But the man in this apartment wants her, wants her more than just the way a client wants her. Perhaps tonight will be the night he sinks to his knees and tells her that he loves her, that he can't be a client anymore, he wants them to go out on real dates: movies, dinners, walks around the seawall.

The thought makes her grin with pleasure, and she tries to focus clearly enough on her reflection to do something about her appearance. Fighting the dizziness from the alcohol, she steadies herself against the counter with the palm of one hand, splashing water over her face. As she straightens up she knocks her forehead against the tap and for a moment the bathroom goes gray, like an old movie. But then the hard surfaces gleam again, the wavy marble of the counter, the stretch of mirror, the faucet. And behind her, a school of fish rises and falls across the shower curtain, circling her head in green and orange halos.

The muffled sound of a cork popping interrupts her as she's tracing a tube of lipstick with exaggerated care across her mouth; it gives her a sense of direction, a place to go. She tugs the bathroom door open and crosses the hall, towards the memory of that sound. He's standing at the kitchen counter, the corkscrew bright and winged in his hand. His mouth exudes the perfume of red wine.

"Sweet Jane," he says.

As she nestles her face against his arm, hair falls into her eyes again, and momentarily the kitchen is seen behind a row of bars and filaments, the counter curving round like a bent dream. She is grateful for this body beside her to hold on to, its limbs more gentle with her than the edges of the counter or the slippery side of the fridge. The wine in her glass catches the overhead light and sends it spinning in thin circles, pretty circles looping between her cupped fingers.

He is kissing her face, her neck, she knows that soon he'll whisper something about the bedroom.

"Wait," she says, pushing at his chest, giggling when he blows once into her ear then lets her go. She crosses the kitchen and then through the living room in her high heels, swaying to the beat of the music video playing from speakers connected to his television. Past the wall-to-wall bookshelves, the stacks of records and CDs, the camera equipment dismantled in the corner, towards the open balcony doors where the cold blows in.

She's lived in this city all her life, nothing is mysterious about its façade beyond the balcony railings — mountains, a few ships in the harbor, the harshly glittering bridges and ski slopes, and the lights of downtown. The lights of the buildings remind her of the apartments where the other men live.

She holds on to the railing and looks down. If she fell the night would glide past her face like a half-remembered dream. Above her the stars have come out in the sky, some fixed, others winking. The sky is hard as slate, but the man in this apartment is soft. He will fix her, make things right. The man is flesh, he has no edges or corners anywhere in his heavy frame. Idly she tries to conjure up the features of his face, but abandons the attempt when she finds she can't, there have been too many other faces. Never mind. She will recognize it when she goes back inside, she'll be able to smile at it and kiss it on the mouth like a lover. If she turns her back now and leaves the balcony, the stars shining fiercely in their flat heavens, she'll be able to pretend the city is a dead thing and that all those lights in all the other apartments are burning in empty rooms.

In the bedroom he's warm, like a pillow she's turned lengthwise and hugged all night into sleep, the way she does at home where she sleeps alone. He smells of detergent and the blue cologne. She regrets that she can't lie in his arms and drink at the same time. From time to time she props herself up on her elbows to swallow from the glass on the bedside table. Its contents no longer taste like anything but cloudy water.

The room itself is cold, he has left the window open upon the hated mountains, the indigo sky. On the cupboard the flames of the oil lamps flicker as though the night is making a wish and trying to blow out all the candles in the man's room. The bed is large and white, like a field of snow. Soon she will have to give him something for his money. Soon she will see his face as if from the end of a tunnel, when he crouches and arranges his limbs above her body.

He is smiling now. He is above her, inside her. The night leaks in through the window, and instead of being with him she remembers all the other male bodies in their apartments bent in supplication or in dominance — her hand raised to push a shoulder down onto a bed or floor, a slender line of blood trailing from a torn nipple. One man struggles with the nozzle of an enema while he fiddles joyfully with his genitals; another lies spread-eagled on a bed, tied with ropes as cleverly wound as the string she played with as a child, making a cradle, making a bridge. Yet another man kneels on a whisky-soaked carpet in an unheated basement, crying and sucking the four-inch heel on her shoe; while in a penthouse one more man carefully removes his black Italian suit to crawl into the foyer, barking like a dog. All their faces are red with pleasure and humiliation and the rage that accompanies their passion. "Please," she wants to whisper, digging her fingernails into this man's arm, "make them go away, make them not real." But the man in the bedroom closes his eyes, he is making love to her between her legs, unaware that she is sweating from the pain of the men around her. Sweat runs from her temples into her open eyes. She tries to count backwards from one hundred: ninety-nine, ninety-eight, make it stop.

The man thinks she is finally feeling pleasure, he is happy, he is smiling so hard she can see his teeth, he too tries to count so he can make it last longer for her: ninety-nine, ninety-eight . . . it goes on for too long, for too long she hears the men scream.

But then it does end. He rolls off her body and stares at her for a moment, his eyes large-pupilled in the candle-light. He lies back with his arms folded behind his head on the bank of white pillows. "Jane," he says, "I think you should leave now."

She drowses all the way home in the taxi, which takes her over the bridge and into the city with its halogen and neon lights alive. The night air is thick as a hangover in her mouth. She sprawls across the back seat, no longer caring about her exposing miniskirt or the driver's contemptuous stare in the rear-view mirror. Across the water the man in his apartment goes to sleep in his white bed.

Jane huddles inside her jacket, her fingers brushing the fifty-dollar bills wedged in a rectangle in her pocket. The downtown streets run together outside, blue and glimmering — storefronts, restaurants, clubs. She leans her forehead against the window, watching beneath her drooping lids the occasional couple sauntering down the street, bits of conversation and a few shrieks of laughter carried to her on the chill wind. Between the waves of nausea it occurs to her that certain things, things that once seemed so possible, are becoming less and less likely with each passing night.

THE OLD MAN

An old man lives across from a restaurant in a neighborhood of art galleries, picture-frame stores, and bookshops. I visit him every other night of the week, at the hour when most families are sitting down to dinner. He watches me pull up the street in a cab whose headlights aim low down the center of the road. Because the interior is dark, he can seldom make out my profile in the back seat, but he knows who it is. He is already waiting with his door open.

Across the street the sign of the restaurant flashes above a panel of stained-glass windows. Usually there are customers entering or leaving, so that the door seems perpetually half-open, and I hear the clink of glasses on trays and glimpse the white jackets the waiters wear. I have never been inside this place, so I do not know if the bursts of laughter come from intimate tables lined against the wall, or from men sitting on barstools with women in short aprons weaving around them, or from round tables of couples and friends. As I leave the cab and turn my back on the restaurant, I hear the tap of women's heels on the cement steps, names being called, and car doors slamming in the dusk.

But I never linger because the old man is waiting. Quickly I step onto the curb and walk across the grass that borders the sidewalk. The stiletto heels of my shoes sharply echo the sounds the restaurant-going women make as I approach the stairs of the building.

As always, the old man is half in shadow and half in light, leaning against the heavy steel door with one shoulder. A triangle of yellow light leaks out from above him and onto the top step. His face is white and retired; he wears a halo of snowy hair that smells of a shampoo with alcohol high on its list of chemicals.

"Barbie," he says. Some nights he calls me Lolita. Or even Cuddles, because he thinks I like to hug him. He is still in the process of naming me; he hasn't found the name that suits me best, he says.

We kiss, and he stops pushing against the door so that it snaps back abruptly on its hinges, hitting me in the back. Once at the end of an evening, as we were waiting for a taxi's headlights to gleam between the parked cars, he accidentally pushed me off the top step and I staggered in my heels, landing at the wrong angle on the step below. Not falling, but twisting my left ankle. He went right on talking, shouldering back the door, hands in his blazer pockets, scanning the string of lights decorating a tree on the street. I had to grip the iron handrail and bite my lip until I could taste a trickle of copper leaking between my teeth. Sometimes he does not seem to notice me; he waved cheerfully when I limped away.

Other times he notices me too well. There are certain unspoken rules which became clear during the first week of our knowing each other. I am never to wear the same complete outfit twice, although if he likes a certain trench coat or short skirt he will be happy to see it again during a different week paired with different accessories. I must always sit with him and drink two double scotches, smiling and engaging him in conversation for no less than an hour but no more than an hour and a half. During this time I should not allow a single moment of contemplative silence to fall between witticisms, praises of him, and news of what I have done in his absence (with the exception of any mentions of other old men). After this I must go to bed with him, although twice a week he will say that this is not necessary, you are probably tired and wish to talk longer or to go home. I pull the corners of my smile up to my temples and say I wish to go to bed with him. Cuddles, he murmurs approvingly. Once when I was feverish and aching from the flu, nauseous from the double Glenfiddichs, I said I *was* tired, but he took my wrists and pulled me into bed and pushed my face between his withered thighs. I was silenced by the strength of the hand circling the back of my neck, its prominent green veins, and the dry creases between the joints of the fingers.

Tonight he follows me down the hallway and into his apartment. He closes the door and pushes a kitchen chair underneath the doorknob. He pulls me to him by the shoulders and directs his tongue into my mouth like an insistent offering of half-cooked meat, faintly gristly and porous. After a while he takes it back and rubs his lips together. I turn and go to my usual place on the couch. He watches me walk and I can tell he is not too happy with my outfit tonight, the red silk shirt and leather skirt, because he only says I am beautiful and wonderfully dressed three times. If I am looking very good, he will say this every five or ten minutes for the rest of the evening. When he does, I must say thank you and keep smiling. This way I end up saying thank you more often than any-thing else when I am with the old man. If I tire of this rou-tine, if instead I only nod or look at him, he will prop his elbows on his knees, lean forward, and ask me intently what is wrong. Then I will say that nothing is wrong, and he will say he does not believe me. And I will insist there is nothing wrong, and then he will point at me with a cal-loused finger and let loose a loud, derisive laugh. I prefer to avoid this. Yet if I arrive in any way dishevelled, or wearing inexpensive clothing, his disapproval clouds the air and makes it thick enough to cut through. He will stare at isolated sections of my body until I want to cover myself in a new designer micro-mini or tear off the mistake of opaque tights in exchange for stay-up stockings with a row of appliqué diamonds running up the left calf.

However, there is the danger of looking too good, and on these few occasions he will combine his attacks by both complimenting me excessively and staring for unblinking minutes at my chest or my knees or the angle at which one shoe is slightly dangling off my foot. He will ask once or twice where I am going after seeing him, all dressed up like that, and he will be looking at the floor when he does this. I will say nowhere, that I dressed up only for him, but he will grunt and refuse to look at my face, as if he is sparing himself from looking full upon a vision of depravity and disease.

Tonight the old man pours the scotch with a generous hand. I measure the inches of pale gold liquid I will have to sip and see there is something paddling about in my drink. It is sort of fibrous and beige and it alternates between suspending itself in the middle of the drink, wafting up to the surface, then sinking with sudden dead weight to the bottom of the glass. I rationalize that I can drink around it until the last gulp, when it will make a quick and, I hope, tasteless exit down the back of my throat.

"How are the girls?" the old man asks, settling himself into the butterfly chair in front of the television. The chair is set in such a way that no matter how I sit on the couch, I cannot comfortably talk to him and face him at the same time. Which, of course, I have to do, resulting in various aches and pains caused by the awkward set of my neck. If I were wearing jeans, I would be able to press my back against one arm of the couch, push the cushions aside, and sit relatively comfortably cross-legged, facing the other arm of the couch. I am not wearing jeans. I have my legs crossed and the glass coffee table is too close to my calves, which I remedy by squashing into the couch and raising my knees unnaturally high.

"Fine," I say, "the girls are fine."

"They're still there, they haven't gone anywhere?"

"They're still there, I take good care of them for you."

The old man chuckles with pleasure. "And the lady, how is she?"

"The lady is fine too."

"Ah," the old man says, rocking back in his chair. "That's good to hear, that's good to hear. Ooh, the lady. Mmm, hum." He rubs his lips together.

Incidentally, the girls are my breasts. The lady is my vagina. I am Barbie, or maybe I am Lolita. For us, the old man has created a secret language, a series of codes and signals, the way lovers do in the early, affectionate, slightly silly phase of their courtship.

"You don't think I'm crazy?" The old man flicks his eyes at the anchorwoman on the television screen then turns them back on me.

"No, I don't think you're crazy."

"Oh, you're just saying that. I am crazy, aren't I? I must be crazy."

"No, not the least bit."

"Not even a little bit crazy?"

"Well, maybe a little bit. Only in the most delightful sort of way." I crack a wide grin at him.

"Ah. Ooh." The old man is pleased with my responses, right on cue. He sets his feet apart on the floor and tugs a bit at his tie. I flatter him by noticing the puffy triangle of silk peeking from his jacket pocket. Thus we settle into our routine, the repetitious dance of compliments and reassurances, of advances and coy retreats, news of the flowers he bought that morning and the phone calls he received and how many times he ate that day and where. I forcefeed myself another mouthful of sullied scotch, keeping a wary eye on the creature snaking in its depths. In the distance, off to one side, he says "You are beautiful, but then there's no need to tell you that, you are always beautiful, aren't you? Aren't you, honey?" and I shake the dizziness out of my head and raise my lips and bare my teeth and say thank you and smile as if my bank balance depended on it.

The old man keeps five blankets on his bed. We make a game of having me wait naked under a different blanket each time I visit. He will creep over to the bed, as he is doing now, in the semi-darkness punctuated by a square of light in the doorway coming from the lamp in the hall. He will shuffle his hands among the layers of wool and cotton, sometimes tickling or pinching me in the process. Tonight I am under blanket number four and it takes him a long time to find me, tossing the first blanket around in the air, attempting to peek under the mattress. When his hand grabs my bare thigh he chuckles and does a little caper of triumph before quickly joining me under the covers.

"Ah, you are a sneaky one, aren't you? Thought you fooled me, didn't you?"

"Yes," I say humbly, "I am very sneaky."

"Hmm? What's that again?"

"It was very sneaky of me to hide like that."

The old man has had enough of the preliminaries, enough foreplay. He pulls me to him by the scruff of my neck and I wrap my arms around his freckled, slightly oily back. He smells of the type of cologne worn by young, muscular men with sculpted hair and faces in magazine ads. Again he shoves his tongue into my mouth; it seems to have doubled in length and thickness since we met at the door. He works it vigorously around my gums for a while. I stroke his grainy back and think of biting his tongue off at the roots. I think of spitting it back into his surprised face, where it will wriggle and twitch before flopping like a small dead trout onto the pillow, oozing blood.

"You do like to kiss and hug, don't you?"

"I like to kiss and hug *you*," I say, pulling back from the tongue that is still disappointingly attached to the blurry old face beside me in bed.

"Cuddles," he says. "You are, aren't you? You're Cuddles," and swiftly he pulls me against him and inserts a cunning leg between my legs. I stifle a small scream as the edge of the metal clasp of his watch accidentally scrapes a few inches of skin off my back, and then another scream as he changes position and in doing so takes another skin sample off my upper arm. Then comes a series of karate jabs, his bony elbows, knees, and shins colliding with soft parts of my body as he tousles with me on the bed, clambering around me and then on top, forgetting to use the mattress instead of my body as a support for his weight.

"Honey," he is saying. "Honey? Please? Please please please please please? Honey? Honey? Can I go in?"

Most of the time he cannot "go in," although he tries. The trying is worse than the "going in." He takes his limpish penis, which I have yet to look at close up, preferring to close my eyes right about now, and attempts to squish, squeeze, prod, bend and otherwise abuse it into place between my thighs. It contorts unhappily, but after a few minutes of what must be agony decides to give up the struggle and go relatively stiff, long enough for it to be inserted, whereupon it instantly falls asleep again. We do not always manage to reach this stage of hasty insertion, but I am always glad when we do because otherwise the fumblings go on for much longer. Once the penis has "gone in" and collapsed, it refuses to be handled again and the evening is over, except for one or two more searing tongue-searches of my tonsils and another soul-crushing hug.

Tonight he enters, goes predictably limp, withdraws wormishly. In the weeks that we have known each other, he has not yet been able to come, although this is evidently what we are striving for. We are making progress; during the first week he had not been able to coax any life whatsoever into his reluctant member.

"Thank you, honey," he breathes into my neck. "Thank you."

"You're welcome."

He takes my chin in his hand and turns my face towards his, moving his arm underneath me. I lose another strip of skin to his watch.

"Thank you," he says meaningfully.

"You're welcome," I repeat, extracting my chin and other body parts and swinging my legs over the side of the bed. I want to hold my head in my hands. I want to run my hands over my body to make an inventory of tonight's damages. What I want to do to the old man, I haven't figured out yet, although the image of the severed tongue flipping about gives me a moment of satisfaction.

"Oh, just you wait," he says from the bed as I cross the room with my clothes in my arms, heading for the bathroom. "One of these days it'll happen, Barbie, bells and whistles will go off. Ooh, just you wait, one of these days I'll blow your head off."

As I hurry to the bathroom I think what a strange image that is for the effect his impending orgasm will have on me. It is almost as if he has picked up that while I was lying there with him I was thinking of blowing my head off, in a rather different context. This is the only time our fantasies join, although even here we mean such different things that we miss each other by fifty years or so.

The old man lives across the street from a trendy restaurant in a popular part of the city. He calls me every other day of the week and I visit him in cabs with drivers who tell me stories of the countries they come from and the holidays they will take once they win the lottery. Some of them know my number, which they pass on to businessmen cabbing downtown from the airport, the ones who are looking to rent someone for an hour or two before a late meeting or dinner with friends. Lately the economy has been bad, business has consequently been slow, and the old man has been my one steady customer, my main squeeze, my man.

I know what will happen from here. There are only so many plot possibilities, only so many combinations of scenarios and outcomes. I expect this old man will be around for another month or two, calling every other day to ask how the girls are doing, and the lady. Fine, I will say, the whole family is doing fine. He will offer to take me away with him for a holiday and we will negotiate a price. We will discuss it over double scotches, planning first-class plane tickets and hotels and what we will bring in our luggage, but we will never go. At some point he will say that he is in love with me. But this will pass, and eventually he will call only every week or two, and then the calls will stop. He may move on to another girl, of a different nationality and with different measurements, or he may meet a woman his age and take her for dinner at the trendy restaurant and move in with her, or most likely he will settle back into his sexless life. I predict he will never blow my head off.

Meanwhile, he is still trying to find the perfect name for me. Barbie, Lolita, Cuddles . . . the old man is not entirely satisfied with any of them. Last night when we were sitting in the living room trying out different names, I slipped in my real one as a suggestion, but he shook his head vigorously. Absolutely not, he said, no way, that isn't you at all.

Also available from Minerva

AMY TAN

The Joy Luck Club

'A brilliant first novel, *The Joy Luck Club* is the story of four mothers and their first-generation Chinese-American daughters; two generations of women struggling to come to terms with their cultural identity. Tan writes from the heart, cutting sharp edges with wit, wisdom and a gentle and delicate precision. From the wealthy homes of pre-revolutionary China to downtown San Francisco and the age of AIDS, the novel covers a remarkable spectrum and reveals the private secrets and ghosts that haunt, torment – and comfort. Completely compelling'
                    Time Out

'In this honest, moving and beautifully courageous story Amy Tan shows us China, Chinese-American women and their families and the mystery of the mother-daughter bond in ways that we have not experienced before'
                    Alice Walker

'Pure enchantment'
                    Mail on Sunday

'In this deft and original début, Amy Tan shows that she is both a consummate storyteller and a writer whose prose manages to be emotionally charged without a trace of sentimentality'
                    Sunday Times

LESLEY GLAISTER

Honour Thy Father

'Wife battering, incest, murder, madness and monstrosity seem a lot to pack into a slim volume but Lesley Glaister's startling short work never gets crowded. This first novel is a true original. Glaister's writing has an earthy grace that takes enrichment from sunshine or corpses. The result is eerie and satisfying – a horror story told with tenderness'
Clare Boylan, *Sunday Times*

'Glaister writes with such accomplishment, indeed mastery, such a gift for character delineation, such an ear for talk'
Ruth Rendell

'This is a remarkable novel, violent and chilling. Black humour fairly drips off the page. Handling poignancy and horror with equal assurance, Glaister deserves attention and applause'
Kirsty Milne, *Sunday Telegraph*

'Witty, macabre and beautifully constructed, it has the makings of a cult book ... I think you should buy a Lesley Glaister book now, before everybody wants one'
Hilary Mantel

'A lovely old-fashioned witches' brew, as choc-a-bloc with nutty hex-appeal as any gothic plum-pudding could be ...'
Valentine Cunningham, *Observer*

IRVINE WELSH

Trainspotting

'An unremitting powerhouse of a novel that marks the arrival of a major new talent. *Trainspotting* is a loosely knotted string of jagged, dislocated tales that lay bare the hearts of darkness of the junkies, wideboys and psychos who ride the down escalator of opportunity in the nation's capital. Loud with laughter in the dark, this novel is the real McCoy. If you haven't heard of Irvine Welsh before . . . don't worry, you will'
The Herald

'A page-turner . . . *Trainspotting* gives the lie to any cosy notions of a classless society'
Independent on Sunday

'The voice of punk, grown up, grown wiser and grown eloquent'
Sunday Times

'A novel perpetually in a starburst of verbal energy – a vernacular spectacular . . . the stories we hear are retched from the gullet'
Scotland on Sunday

'*Trainspotting* marks the capital début of a capital writer. This marvellous novel might feel like a bad day in Bedlam, but boy is it exhilarating'
Jeff Torrington

A. L. KENNEDY

Looking for the Possible Dance

'This beautiful novel is the story of Margaret and the two men in her life: her father, who brought her up, and Colin, her lover . . . A tender, moving story, punctuated by flashes of comedy and one climactic moment of appalling violence'
Literary Review

'A writer rich in the humanity and warmth that seems at a premium in these bleak times'
Salman Rushdie

'Praise the Lord and pass the orchids – a *real* writer is among us, with a beautiful first novel'
Julie Burchill

'An austere and intense talent . . . A. L. Kennedy turns pointlessness into significance'
Sunday Telegraph

'Here is the most promising of the rich new crop of Scottish writers'
Scotsman

'A novel of undeniable warmth and charm'
Jonathan Coe, *Guardian*

ALBERT FRENCH

Billy

The tale of Billy Lee Turner, a ten-year-old boy
convicted for the murder of a white girl in Mississippi
in 1937, illuminates the monstrous face of racism in
America with harrowing clarity and power. Narrated in
the rich accents of the American South, Billy's story is
told amidst the picking-fields and town streets, the heat,
dust and poverty of the region in the time of the
Depression. Albert French's haunting first novel is a
story of racial injustice, as unsentimental as it is
heartbreaking.

'I kept trying to think of a writer who has done a better
job of capturing clear, powerful and authentic language,
the landscape, the people ... the air itself. I kept
searching for comparisons and I kept coming up with
masters of the art, from Aeschylus to Ernest Gaines'
David Bradley

'*Billy* is a book that will stay with me in my dreams'
Tim O'Brien

ALINA REYES

The Butcher

A young girl goes to work in a butcher's shop during her college holiday. Every day the butcher whispers obscenities in her ear, describing their imagined lovemaking. And as the summer heat takes hold, so does her lust . . .

'Nothing short of staggering . . . an erotic *tour de force*; an exploration of raw sensuality – fleshy, beautiful and obscene. When you put it down, exhausted, you know you want to read it again'
Evening Standard

'This is not eroticism or soft-focus four-poster-bed sex. It is pornography, pure and simple. Utterly, absolutely, sexy . . . *The Butcher* has that crafted, stylised quality which compels the reader to linger and is another magnificent touch in the explosive build up of sexual tension. Its contents are guaranteed to disturb, unnerve and grip you; you will want to read it again and again'
Literary Review

'I never knew such goings-on were even possible in a freezer . . . this is eroticism on a fantasy level which just about saves the book from obscenity. I think. But you have been warned'
Daily Express

Edited by GILES GORDON
and DAVID HUGHES

The Minerva Book of
Short Stories 5

'Ideal for the beach or the train journey, providing
postcard-like glimpses of fictional places one might
choose to revisit – or to avoid . . . Here the reader may
pass from the dystopian landscapes of Brian Aldiss into
the stifling atmosphere of nineteenth-century England,
as delineated by Angela Carter. Moving on (pausing
only to sign the visitor's book in Stephen Gallagher's
haunted holiday cottage), the reader travels through the
vistas of post-war Japan offered by Steven Heighton's
elegiac story, to the Australian outback depicted by
Janette Turner Hospital, to Jonathan Treitel's
turn-of-the-century Vienna or – more exotic still – to
Salman Rushdie's fifteenth-century Spain. A number of
the stories included here contrive to suggest not simply
a landscape but an entire world'

Christina Koning, *The Times*

ROBERT OLEN BUTLER

A Good Scent from a Strange Mountain

'The book has attracted such acclaim not simply because it is beautifully and powerfully written, but because it convincingly pulls off an immense imaginative risk . . . Butler has not entered the significant and ever-growing canon of Vietnam-related fiction (he has long been a member) – he has changed its composition for ever'
Guardian

'It is the Vietnamese voice that Butler seeks and that, in these stories, he has so remarkably and movingly found'
Los Angeles Times

'Delicately moving . . . Each of the fifteen stories brings us a sharp impression of a different person, speaking magically to us across the silent page'
New York Newsday

'Funny and deeply affecting . . . One of the strongest collections I've read in ages'
Ann Beattie

Further Short Story Collections Available from Minerva

☐	7493 9119 7	**Sixty Stories**	Donald Barthelme	£6.99
☐	7493 9933 3	**Collected Short Stories**	Bertolt Brecht	£5.99
☐	7493 9767 5	**A Good Scent From A Strange Mountain**	Robert Olen Butler	£5.99
☐	7493 9967 8	**Difficult Loves**	Italo Calvino	£5.99
☐	7493 9968 6	**The Minerva Book of Short Stories 5**	Giles Gordon and David Hughes	£5.99
☐	7493 9949 X	**The Burn**	James Kelman	£5.99
☐	7493 9706 3	**Lipstick on the Host**	Aidan Mathews	£5.99
☐	7493 9113 8	**Lust & Other Stories**	Susan Minot	£4.99
☐	7493 9853 1	**New Writing 2**	Malcolm Bradbury and Andrew Motion	£6.99
☐	7493 9748 9	**New Writing 3**	Andrew Motion and Candice Rodd	£6.99
☐	7493 9162 6	**Four Bare Legs in a Bed**	Helen Simpson	£4.99